W9-AZB-117

Cinders
and
Sparks

GOBLINS AND GOLD

Books by Lindsey Kelk

The fantastic Cinders and Sparks adventures
in reading order:

MAGIC AT MIDNIGHT
FAIRIES IN THE FOREST
GOBLINS AND GOLD

Cinders and Sparks

GOBLINS AND GOLD

LINDSEY KELK

Illustrated by Pippa Curnick

HarperCollins *Children's Books*

First published in Great Britain by
HarperCollins *Children's Books* in 2020
HarperCollins *Children's Books* is a division of HarperCollins*Publishers* Ltd,
HarperCollins Publishers
1 London Bridge Street
London SE1 9GF

The HarperCollins website address is
www.harpercollins.co.uk

1

Text copyright © Lindsey Kelk 2020
Illustrations copyright © Pippa Curnick 2020
Cover design copyright © HarperCollins*Publishers* Ltd 2020
All rights reserved.

ISBN 978-0-00-829217-1

Lindsey Kelk and Pippa Curnick assert the moral right to be identified
as the author and illustrator of the work respectively.
A CIP catalogue record for this title is available from the British Library.

Typeset in Stempel Garamond Roman 13pt/24pt
Printed and bound in England by CPI Group (UK) Ltd, Croydon, CR0 4YY

Conditions of Sale
This book is sold subject to the condition that it shall not, by way of trade
or otherwise, be lent, re-sold, hired out or otherwise circulated without
the publisher's prior consent in any form, binding or cover other than that
in which it is published and without a similar condition including this
condition being imposed on the subsequent purchaser.

MIX
Paper from
responsible sources
www.fsc.org **FSC™ C007454**

This book is produced from independently certified FSC™ paper
to ensure responsible forest management.

For more information visit: www.harpercollins.co.uk/green

For Princess Penny.
If you could wish for anything,
what would it be?

Chapter One

Cinders was a girl with a lot on her mind. Here she was, trotting through a forest on a horse that used to be a mouse, with her best friend, who just so happened to be a talking dog, and a boy in a green hat named Hansel. But she wasn't thinking about any of them. She was thinking about her mum, her dad and a little bit about where they

were going to get their lunch.

'You're very quiet,' Hansel said from the back
of Mouse the horse.

'Am I?' Cinders replied.

'I don't like it when you're quiet,' Hansel said.
'It's weird.'

'Don't get used to it,' Sparks piped up from
his spot in front of Cinders, his head nestled in
Mouse's mane. 'I think this is the longest she's
gone without

speaking since she learned to talk.'

'What if Hansel is right?' Cinders began. 'What if my mum was the princess who went missing from Fairyland all those years ago?'

Sparks sighed. *There goes my peace and quiet*, he thought to himself.

The four friends were on a quest. Cinders had recently found that she could do magic and it turned out it was because her mother had been a fairy. Unfortunately, she couldn't ask her mother about that because she had died soon after Cinders was born, and she couldn't ask her father because he was back at home in the kingdom. The kingdom was the one place Cinders definitely could not return to because the king hated magic, and would throw her in

the dungeons for sure. Mostly because of an accidental wish-granting incident that saw King Picklebottom bitten on the bottom by a roast pig Cinders had not-at-all-on-purpose brought back to life.

The king hated magic, which meant the king hated Cinders. It was all quite a mess.

'It was just an idea,' Hansel said, scratching

his hair underneath his hat. 'Although I am very
often right about things.'

(He wasn't.)

Hansel had joined the quest after helping
himself to one too many delicious tiles from
the roof of his neighbour's gingerbread house.
Mouse had joined the quest after Cinders
turned him into a horse and he found he quite
liked it. Sparks had joined the quest because
Cinders was his best friend and, even if she was
quite loud, occasionally annoying and never
packed enough sausages, he loved her more
than anything.

'Besides,' Hansel said, 'surely you'd know if
your mum was a fairy princess. Wouldn't you
have extra-extra-special powers or something?'

'You mean something like magical, sparkly fingers that make wishes come true?' Cinders suggested. 'And let's not forget that time I flew.'

'I'm not sure floating thirty centimetres off the ground counts as flying,' Sparks said with a gruffly yawn. 'I've got an idea – why don't you wish up some lunch? I'm getting hungry.'

That was hardly a surprise. Sparks was almost always starving.

'I don't think I'll have to,' Cinders said. She gave the air a big sniff. 'Can you smell that?'

'Freshly baked bread!' Hansel gasped. His mouth began to water. 'Oh, what I wouldn't give for a nice slice of toast.'

'Come on, Mouse, let's go and find something to eat.' Cinders flicked the reins and Mouse

picked up speed, galloping through the forest, following the delicious aromas that wafted towards them.

For the first time in ages, the twisted tree trunks of the Dark Forest parted and Cinders could see the blue sky overhead. And not just the sky, but beyond the line of the forest she saw a towering mountain in the distance, fields full of pink grass and colourful houses dotted along a blue-bricked road. At the end of the road was a market.

'I don't want to exaggerate,' Sparks said, sitting up in Cinders's lap, 'but this might be the most excited I have ever been. Markets almost always mean sausages.'

'Agreed,' said Cinders as they clip-clopped

on to the blue bricks. 'Let's go and find some snacks!'

In no time at all, they arrived at the market. Even though it looked like any other market from a distance, close up Cinders could tell it was somehow different. The stalls were brightly coloured, gleaming cascades of silk covered the tables and stands, and the air was filled with the sweetest smells. The market stalls in the kingdom all used rough canvas or white cotton to cover their stands and, no matter what day of the week it was, all Cinders could ever smell was fish and Cinders hated the smell of fish.

Neither Sparks nor Hansel were able to do magic themselves, but, if they could have granted a wish or two, they would have

magicked something very much like the food they found at the very first market stall. Big, plump, juicy sausages for Sparks, freshly baked cakes for Cinders and, well, Hansel wasn't fussy. He would happily eat anything.

'Everything looks delicious,' Cinders said, her mouth watering.

'It does,' Hansel agreed, looking round the marketplace. 'But are we sure it's safe to eat? I don't think these people are quite like us.'

Cinders looked up from a particularly appealing sweet stall that sold seventeen different flavours of fudge.

'What do you mean?' she asked.

'Look,' Hansel whispered, nodding at a man walking by. 'They're weird.'

The person in question was much shorter than Cinders or Hansel and his skin was a very pale purple colour. His spiky hair was bright green and his big, smiling eyes were such a bold yellow that Cinders was certain she'd be able to see them in the dark.

'They just look different to us, that's all,' Cinders said, her own eyes again fixed firmly on the fudge. 'Not everyone's the same.'

'I suppose so,' Hansel replied. She had a point. Up until a couple of days ago, he'd never met a dog that could talk, but Sparks wasn't weird. A bit rude sometimes, but that was just Sparks.

'Excuse me,' Cinders said to the blue-haired lady behind the fudge counter.

She turned and gasped, looking Cinders up and down in surprise.

Hmm, Cinders thought, *Hansel isn't the only one who thinks certain people here look odd. They're as confused by us as we are by them!*

'How much is your vanilla-strawberry-chocolate-chip fudge?'

'All the fudge is one gold piece per bag,' the lady replied, eyeing the group curiously. It wasn't often they saw people from the kingdom beyond the Dark Forest. In fact, she had only ever met one person from there before in her entire life and she hoped never to run into him again. She shivered, thinking of his big black hood and big black boots.

'Thank you very much,' Cinders said with a

huge smile before turning back to her friends.

'Okay, the fudge is one gold piece per bag. Hansel, how much money have you got with you?'

'Absolutely none,' he replied.

'And I've got –' Cinders dug her hands deep into her pockets – 'a button. Flipping fiddlesticks! How are we going to buy something to eat if we don't have the money to pay for it?'

'Um, Cinders,' Sparks said, pointing to a poster with his front paw. 'I think we might have a bigger problem right now.'

Cinders gasped.

Nailed to the tree behind her was a wanted poster.

A wanted poster with her picture on it!

Chapter Two

*E*ven the bravest prince in the entire
world might have been a little bit nervous
riding through the Dark Forest on his own, and
Prince Joderick Jorenson Picklebottom was the
first to admit he was hardly the bravest prince
in the entire world. Joderick was the kind of
prince who would much rather spend his days
baking a perfect chocolate soufflé or playing

22

video games. But here he was, riding his horse, Muffin, through the darkest part of the Deep Dark Very Incredibly Scary Forest, looking for his friend Cinders.

'So . . . which way do you think we should go?' Joderick asked Muffin as they came to a fork in the trail.

Muffin snorted in response. She wasn't magic like Sparks, so she couldn't tell him what she

thought. And, if she could, she didn't think he would appreciate her response very much anyway.

Joderick looked down at the map he had secretly borrowed-without-asking from his father's private desk, and frowned at the big tear that ran right down the edge. Joderick must have ripped it when he pulled it out of the desk, and now he had reached the end of the trail marked out on the parchment. He had no idea where to go next.

'Why is it, whenever I bump into people from the kingdom, they're always hanging around like spare parts?'

Joderick looked up from his map to see a woman standing right in front of him. He

blinked and rubbed his eyes. Where had she come from? She wasn't there a minute ago. And he couldn't help but notice that her hair was very red and her skin was very pale and, if he wasn't much mistaken, she had a pair of quite impressive wings sprouting out of the middle of her back.

'Giddy gumdrops,' Joderick whispered. 'You're a fairy.'

'I'm not getting anything past you, am I?' she replied. 'What's wrong with you? Never seen a fairy before?'

'A-actually, n-no,' he said, stuttering over every word. 'Fairies are banned from the kingdom. Are you going to eat me?'

That did it. The fairy started laughing as

though Hansel had said the funniest thing she'd ever heard. She laughed so hard, she fell to the ground with a hard **PLOp!**, tears streaming from her eyes and fogging up her glasses. (Yes, some fairies do need glasses. Just because they can grant wishes and fly doesn't mean they have perfect eyesight.)

'Eat you?' the fairy gasped, clutching her sides. The prince had made her laugh so hard, she'd given herself a stitch. 'I shouldn't think so.

Can you imagine the mess? And there's hardly any meat on those bones anyway. I'm a fairy with a good appetite, and you wouldn't fill up a flea.'

'Right,' Joderick said, still wary of the red-headed lady.

Ever since he was a teeny-tiny little baby, his mother and father had told him stories of how evil the fairies were. How they stalked children at night, how they crept around with long claws and sharp teeth, and how they were determined to take over the kingdom. But this fairy didn't have long claws or sharp teeth, and she certainly didn't seem very interested in eating him. In fact, she'd already pulled a cupcake out of her bag and was happily tucking into that instead.

'I'm looking for a girl,' the fairy said, a dollop of icing on the end of her nose. 'About your height, fair hair, very messy, probably covered in muck and with food all over her face.'

Joderick's eyes widened.

'You wouldn't be talking about Cinders by any chance, would you?' he asked.

'How do you know my goddaughter?' the fairy replied.

'She's my friend. I'm looking for her too,' Joderick said, completely gobsmacked. 'You're

Cinders's godmother?'

'Yes.'

'But you're a fairy!'

'Sharpest knife in the drawer, aren't you, clever clogs?' Brian muttered to herself. 'Yes, I'm Cinders's godmother and yes, I'm a fairy and, as I mentioned, I'm looking for her. Have you seen her or not because I'm in something of a rush. There's a very large man with a very large axe roaming around these woods who is also looking for her and I'd much prefer it if I found her first.'

All the colour drained from Joderick's face.

'I really, really, really, really hope you aren't talking about the Huntsman,' he said, holding Muffin's reins a little bit tighter.

'That's him,' Brian said with a chuckle.
'Fancies himself a bit, doesn't he?'

Joderick was very pleased to be up on his
horse because he was shaking so much that, if
he'd been down on the ground, Brian would
have seen his knees knocking together.

'The Huntsman is the most feared man in
the entire kingdom,' he said in a wobbly voice.
'He has never failed to complete a mission.
Whatever he hunts, he catches. He isn't scared
of anything.'

Brian shrugged. 'Everyone is scared of
something. For me, it's guinea pigs. I don't like
their little hands . . .'

'I'm serious!' Joderick told her, trying not
to sound too wibbly. 'Anything you tell

him to find, he finds it. And I don't think
he always asks nicely.'

He knew his father would say it wasn't very
becoming for a prince to sound so scared, but
they were talking about the Huntsman, and he
was after Cinders.

'I don't know what you're so worried
about,' Brian said, fluttering her wings until
she was up on her feet once again. 'Like I said,
everyone is afraid of something, and I happen
to have an inkling of what will scare him.'

'What are you, some sort of mind-reader?'
Joderick asked.

'Yes,' she replied confidently.

Joderick wasn't sure if she was being serious
or not, but she very much looked like she was.

'The bigger they come, the harder they fall,' Brian went on. 'Besides, all we have to do is find Cinders first and then we needn't worry about him.'

'And how are we going to do that?' Joderick asked.

She looked at him with a little smile on her shining face.

'Magic,' she said, snapping her fingers.

And, just like that, they both

disappeared.

Chapter Three

'*Okay, here's the plan.*'

Cinders, Hansel, Sparks and Mouse all huddled together in a circle.

'I'm going to wish for some gold. As soon as it appears, Hansel, you grab it and go to the sausage stall and buy us all some lunch,' Cinders instructed, wiggling her fingers to warm them up. 'Sparks, you go with Hansel

and make sure he gets the right stuff and doesn't draw attention to himself while me and Mouse hide back here.'

'Oi,' Hansel said, looking a little hurt. 'I can be trusted to buy a sausage, you know.'

Sparks and Cinders shared a look.

'Are you even sure you can wish up some gold?' Hansel asked. 'Your wishes haven't always gone according to plan . . .'

He wasn't exactly wrong. There was the pig that had bitten the king on the bottom, and that one time she'd accidentally magicked up a munklepoop when they were lost in the forest, not to mention the time she'd accidentally frozen Sparks in mid-air.

'No time to worry about that,' Cinders said,

ignoring Hansel. She was getting quite
good at ignoring Hansel.

She crouched down behind Mouse who shook
out his mane in a very nonchalant manner. Or
as nonchalant a manner as possible for a horse
that used to be a mouse. It was quite hard not
to draw attention to yourself when you looked
different to everyone else, and Cinders, Mouse
and Hansel looked very, very different.

'I wish we had some gold to buy lunch.'

She was still really quite new at doing magic
and, every time Cinders's fingers started
to tingle, she got a little bit excited

and a tiny bit nervous. What if something went wrong? What if Sparks turned to gold? What if a giant gold bar appeared out of nowhere and squished them all flat like pancakes? But they needed to eat, and to eat they needed gold, and this was the only way she could think to get some. Cinders could hardly offer to do chores in exchange for food when there were wanted posters all over the market with her face on them. Plus, she really, really hated doing chores.

'Here we go,' Sparks said, crouching his head down low and sticking his doggy bottom up high, ready to leap up and protect his best friend.

Hansel, Mouse and Sparks all watched as shimmering shots of silver and gold began to

flicker from Cinders's hands before glittery sparkles ran all the way up her arms and down her back, until her whole body was glowing.

'I will never get used to this,' Hansel gasped.

'How do you think I feel?' Cinders asked him as she began to float up off the ground.

Just when she thought she was going to fly all the way up to the sky, a tiny white cloud appeared over her head and it began to rain. It began to rain shiny gold coins.

'Ow!' Cinders exclaimed, covering her head with her hands as the coins kept coming. Hansel scrambled to pick them up as they fell to the ground, rolling around at their feet.

'Good work, Cinders!' he exclaimed, stuffing his pockets full. 'You're getting better at this!'

'Thank you,' she replied, rubbing a sore spot on the top of her noggin. 'Now it's your turn to make yourself useful.'

Hansel did not need telling twice. Scooping up another handful of magical coins, he and Sparks raced off into the market, leaving Cinders and Mouse to lurk quietly on the edges.

'If my mum was a fairy, then I'm half fairy too,' she said, looking Mouse squarely in the eye.

He squeaked in agreement.

'But Rapunzel said fairies can talk to animals,' she added. 'And not just Sparks because he can talk to anyone. I should be able to talk to you, Mouse.'

Mouse cocked his head to one side.

'It would be nice to know what you're thinking,' Cinders sighed. 'Almost as nice as it would be to find out who my mother really was.'

'Hello, there!'

Cinders turned round quickly. She was sure she'd heard someone say something, but she couldn't see anyone.

'Down here,' the voice said.

She dipped her head and saw a short, stout man standing in front of her. He had silver-grey hair and a tall, pointy hat on his head. He looked very kind with shining violet eyes, a large nose and a big beaming smile underneath a long grey beard that stopped somewhere near his knees.

'Hello,' he said again. 'Were you just talking to your horse?'

'Absolutely not,' Cinders replied nervously. So much for not drawing attention to herself. 'What sort of weirdo would talk to a horse?'

'I don't know,' the man chuckled, stroking his beard. 'You might get more sense out of a horse than some of the folks around these parts.'

Cinders smiled. He seemed nice enough and she missed nice people. He even reminded her a little bit of her dad, and she missed him most of all.

'I was just having a chat with your pal back by the sausage stall,' the man went on. 'He said you were looking for some lunch?'

'Did he now?' she asked, looking out into the market for blabbermouth Hansel.

'He did indeed.' The little man nodded. 'So I sent him and the dog back to my restaurant for a slap-up sausage feast. If you'd care to join us, I could walk you over myself?'

Before Cinders could say anything, her stomach rumbled so loudly that the man guffawed, clutching his belly with joy.

'Blummin' blumkins, would you listen to that? You must be starved!' he said, still laughing. 'No wonder your friends were after the biggest, juiciest sausages in the market.'

42

Just the thought of a sausage made Cinders's mouth water.

'Hansel and Sparks are already at the restaurant?' she asked.

'They are indeed,' the man replied. 'Probably tucking into their first plump porker as we speak.'

Cinders looked at Mouse. Mouse looked at Cinders. He didn't seem completely convinced by this stout little man, but he was also a horse that used to be a mouse, so she wasn't sure that he knew what he was on about anyway. Besides, she was very hungry and it seemed as though it might be a good idea to get out of the market square and away from those wanted posters.

'All right,' she said, sticking her hands in her pockets and giving the man a grin. 'Where's your restaurant?'

'Right this way,' he said with a huge smile on his face. 'Follow me and don't worry about a thing . . .'

Chapter Four

A long, long, long way away, Joderick's father, King Poderick Porenson Picklebottom, was not thinking about Cinders or Joderick, or even the Huntsman. He was sitting on his throne, playing a game on his mobile phone. The queen sat beside him on a throne of her own, reading a book she'd been looking forward to for ages. She wasn't exactly

thrilled that Joderick had gone missing, but it was nice to have a bit of time to herself.

'Your Majesties!'

The doors to the throne room flew open and two pages appeared, flanked by four of the king's guards.

King Picklebottom held up one finger for everyone to be quiet while he finished his game.

'Score!' he yelled happily before turning his attention to the pages. 'Now,

what have you got for me?'

'We have news—' began the first page.

'About your son,' finished the second.

'Have you found him?' the king asked.

'No,' said the second page.

'But he was spotted,' added the first.

'By a baby bear,' they chorused.

'And did this baby bear provide any proof?' the king asked, looking back at his phone.

He was getting good at this game. If only he could manage one hour of the day without any interruptions, he might finally be able to get up to the next level.

'No, Your Majesty,' the pages confirmed as one.

'Then he's not getting the reward,' the king grumbled. Ever since they announced Joderick was missing, he'd been spotted everywhere – down the supermarket, up a beanstalk, living in a shoe. It was all a complete load of tosh.

'We believe the bear is telling the truth,' said the first page.

'He said the prince was looking for a girl called Cinders,' said the second.

At last, the king put down his phone and the queen looked up from her book.

'Cinders? CINDERS?' King Picklebottom leaped out of his throne with a roar. 'What else did he say?'

'He said his mum offered the prince a sandwich,' began the second page.

'And sent him on his way,' finished the first.

The queen gripped the arms of her throne so tightly, her fingers turned white.

'Did they say what kind of sandwich?' she asked.

'It doesn't matter what kind of sandwich!' the king bellowed.

'Yes it does,' argued his wife. 'Joderick likes his cheese sandwiches cut into triangles with no crusts, but, if it's a ham sandwich, he likes the crusts left on and cuts it into squares and, if it's a tuna sandwich, he'd much prefer it in a roll—'

'That's quite enough about sandwiches,' the king declared as the four guards looked at each other hungrily. It was ages since breakfast and they all fancied a sandwich. 'Where are these bears?'

The first page answered the king. 'In the Dark Forest.'

And the second page added, 'Near the Alabaster Tower.'

The king gulped. It was a long time since he'd heard talk of the Alabaster Tower. And even longer since he'd seen it.

'There's nothing to worry about,' he insisted, resting back against his throne and putting on a brave face. 'The Huntsman will find both Prince Joderick and that girl in no time.

Now, who fancies a cup of tea?'

The queen didn't look quite as confident as the king sounded, but she also really wanted to get back to her book.

'If you're sure, dear,' she said, flicking through the book to find her page. 'I hope he's back by teatime. I don't like the sound of my son accepting sandwiches from strange bears.'

'I'm sure he will be, I'm sure he will be,' said the king, waving the pages away and going back to his game.

But there was someone else listening in the hallway. Someone who was not quite as sure about things as the king appeared to be.

Margery, Cinders's stepmother, curtsied at the guards and the pages as they trooped down the

hallway, away from the throne room.

'We need Joderick to come home to the palace and we need Cinders to stay far away,' she said, speaking quietly to her dutiful daughters, Elly and Aggy. They were close behind her, as always.

'We do,' agreed Aggy.

'We do?' echoed Elly. 'Why's that?'

'Because, if the prince doesn't come back, how can he fall in love with one of you and make you his queen?' Margery replied.

'I don't know,' Elly replied, puzzled. 'Is that what we want?'

'It is,' her mother insisted.

'It is,' Aggy agreed. She was quite excited about the idea of being queen. She'd already seen a nice white dress with lots of ruffles at the shoulders and it had royal wedding written all over it.

Her younger sister still looked a little confused.

'But how will you convince Prince Joderick he wants to marry me or Aggy if he's already decided he wants to marry Cinders?' she asked.

Margery smirked and tightened the bow in her youngest daughter's hair, pulling until Elly squealed.

'You leave that with me,' she said. 'Just you leave that with me.'

Chapter Five

'*This is a very odd spot for a restaurant,*' Cinders said, following the little man with the pointy hat and long grey beard down a dark alleyway.

Behind her, Mouse squeaked in agreement, trotting after her down the narrow passageway as quickly as he could.

'It's a secret restaurant,' the man replied,

opening a small, square door at the end of the alley. 'If everyone knew about it, there wouldn't be any sausages left for you and your friends.'

'Fair enough.'

The door was so small, Cinders had to get down on her hands and knees to shuffle inside. Mouse stood watching her with interest.

'It's awfully dark in here,' she called back.

'That's to keep everyone else away,' he explained. 'You don't need to be able to see to eat sausages, do you?'

It was a good point. Cinders was so hungry, she could have eaten sausages with her eyes closed and her hands tied behind her back. She wondered what her stepmother would have to say about that. It probably wouldn't be

considered very good manners.

'And these metal bars?' Cinders asked, feeling her way around. 'What are those for?'

'Those bars are to keep you trapped inside, of course,' the man replied gleefully, slamming the door shut with a loud *CLANG!*

Mouse gave a loud yelp and sped off, cantering in the direction of the marketplace.

'Trapped?' Cinders grabbed the bars and rattled hard, but they didn't budge. 'Why would you trap me?'

She blinked as her eyes became accustomed to the light of the room – this wasn't a restaurant at all! It was just a small, dark and dingy house and there wasn't a single sausage in sight.

'I saw you wishing up gold out of thin air,' the

man said, the friendly smile vanishing from his face. 'Now you're going to wish some up for me. You're going to wish for more gold than anyone could ever imagine and make me the richest goblin that ever lived!'

So he was a goblin. Cinders had very much hoped their bad reputation had been exaggerated, but clearly not. The short stature, the silly beard, the tiny hands . . . she should have known.

'I wish I was out of this house!' Cinders yelled, closing her eyes and concentrating as hard as she could. 'I wish I was back in the market with Hansel and Sparks and Mouse!'

She opened her eyes but nothing happened, so she tried again.

'I wish I was back in the market RIGHT NOW!'

Still nothing happened.

'You can keep going,' the goblin chuckled, stroking his long grey beard, 'but this house is just as magic as you are. It won't let you wish for anything other than gold.'

Cinders bit her lip. That was not good news.

'My friends will come and find me,' she said, quite certain she was right. Sparks would know she was in trouble and Hansel might be a bit rubbish from time to time, but he definitely wouldn't leave her trapped with a goblin.

'How will your friends know where you are?' the little man asked. 'No one saw you come with me apart from that weird horse of yours,

and although he's run off he can't exactly tell
anyone, can he?'

Cinders was stumped. Stumped and stuck.
The little man did a dance of glee round the
room, his long, pointed slippers slapping against
the flagstones. And then Cinders had an idea.

'It's just such a shame,' she said with a
big sigh, 'that all my wishes seem to undo

themselves at midnight. So any gold I wish for will disappear at the end of the day.'

The goblin stopped dancing and stared at the messy-haired girl.

'Are you fibbing?' he asked, narrowing his eyes to peer at her through the bars.

'My dad taught me never to fib,' she replied.

'Well, that does change things,' he said. 'I suppose you'll have to stay here forever.'

Cinders gasped. Well, that plan certainly backfired.

'There has to be a way to settle this,' she pleaded, giving him her sweetest smile. 'Surely you wouldn't really keep someone trapped forever and ever just so you can collect masses of gold.'

'Oh, no, I wouldn't keep someone just to

collect gold,' he agreed. 'I intend to spend it on really cool stuff. Have you seen the latest FunStation? It's got the best computer games ever! And, as soon as you start wishing for my gold, I'm going out to buy one.'

Cinders slumped down where she stood. There would be no wishing or talking her way out of this one.

'There is one way to get out of the room,' the goblin said with a mischievous grin. 'If you can guess the magic word, it'll break the spell.'

'Will you give me a clue?' she asked hopefully.

'Certainly,' he cackled. 'The magic word is my name! Guess my name and you will be free. Until then, you'd better get wishing!'

Chapter Six

When Joderick and Brian popped out of mid-air and landed in the middle of the market, no one batted an eyelid. Brian fluttered her wings, floating down to the ground gracefully while the prince fell right on his bum.

'Where's Muffin?' Joderick asked, rubbing his rump. His horse was nowhere to be seen.

'Oh, I sent her home,' Brian replied, tightening

the orange shoelaces on her pink trainers. 'She wanted to be back in her stable by dinnertime, and I couldn't quite see that happening.'

Joderick wasn't sure what was more alarming: the fact that this fairy had had a conversation with his horse, or the fact that he was on track to miss his next meal.

'Look at all these strange people,' he whispered, gazing round the marketplace. He didn't get out of the palace very often and, when he did, he was almost always with his family and the royal guards, which meant he saw practically nothing.

Brian looked at him, a little bit confused.

'Strange? How are they strange?'

'Well, you know . . .' Joderick pointed at a green-skinned man with purple hair as he trotted by, walking a pink-and-yellow striped cat on a lead. 'They're all so . . . different.'

'Different to you,' Brian replied. 'Everyone here is as colourful as a rainbow. To them, you're the strange one. Boring, to be honest. Have you ever thought about doing something fun with your hair?'

The prince gulped as he noticed more and more people giving him shifty looks. He was a prince – he was used to being stared at – but normally people were cheering his name and taking his picture. Here, in this odd market

square, no one looked especially pleased to see
him. He stuck out like a sore thumb.

'Maybe they wouldn't be staring if you weren't
wearing that ridiculous neckerchief,' Brian said,
nodding towards Joderick's ruff. 'What's the
point of it anyway? It looks like you've thrown
a lace doily round your neck. I wouldn't be
surprised if someone mistook you for a table and
tried to place a cup of tea on your head!'

Sheepishly, Joderick tugged on his collar.

'Or maybe they're looking at me because
of that,' he said, pointing across the way and
gulping with fear.

Hanging right next to one of Cinderella's
wanted posters was a huge piece of parchment,
inscribed with the words:

MISSING!

PRINCE JODERICK JORENSON PICKLEBOTTOM,
PRINCE OF THE REALM AND EXTREMELY
HANDSOME YOUNG MAN.
REWARD: 100 GOLD PIECES.

'I never should have brought you,' Brian went on, muttering to herself. 'No one is going to help me find that goddaughter of mine with you trailing around behind me. And honestly! Extremely handsome? I'm not sure about that, Noderick.'

'It's Joderick,' Joderick replied, not sure whether to be offended or not.

'I like Noderick,' Brian said. 'And I think we should send you home.'

But the prince wasn't ready to give up just yet.

'No!' he exclaimed. 'I really want to help Cinders. She's the best friend I've ever had. I can't just let the Huntsman catch her.'

Brian considered the young man. He seemed truthful enough, and it was very brave of him to trot out into the Dark Forest all on his own, but any one of these market traders would happily turn him in for a hundred gold pieces, and that would only make her job more complicated.

'Do you think there's something you could do to help me blend in?' Joderick asked as a man rode by on a purple polka-dot giraffe. 'Perhaps a disguise of some kind?'

'I thought you'd never ask,' Brian said with a grin. 'Let's have a go, shall we?'

With a flick of her wrist, a cloud of gold and silver glitter whirled round him like a tiny tornado, covering him up from the tip of his toes to the top of his head.

'How do I look?' he asked as the sparkles began to settle on the floor.

Brian stepped back to admire her handiwork.

'I don't see you winning any beauty contests, but you'll pass,' she said, fishing around in a handbag she produced from nowhere to pull

out a mirror that couldn't possibly have fitted inside. 'Whaddya think?'

Joderick couldn't believe it. The face staring back from the mirror was still his, but now his skin was a very fetching shade of navy blue, his eyes were neon green and his hair shone silver and gold in the sunshine. He looked up at the people bustling around him and no one in the marketplace gave him so much as a second glance.

'I like it,' he said as Brian slid the huge mirror back into the tiny bag. 'Now, where shall we start looking for Cinders?'

'Anywhere but here,' Brian said, grabbing hold of Joderick's arm and dragging him away from the middle of the square and off behind a stand selling dozens of different delicious-smelling cakes that made Joderick's mouth water.

'What's wrong?' he asked as Brian pulled a very large pair of sunglasses out of her bag and put them on over the top of her normal glasses.

'See that chap over there?' she hissed, pointing at a short man with a very long grey beard, wearing a tall, pointed hat.

Joderick nodded.

'I went to school with him and he's the worst,'

she said. 'Total braggart, always going on about how brilliant he is. Haven't the time to deal with that particular goblin today.'

Ooh, a goblin! thought Joderick, craning his neck to get a better look. He'd never seen a goblin before. In fact, he hadn't even thought they were real until now. Fairies, goblins, talking bears . . . he was starting to wonder what other kinds of creature he was going to meet on this adventure.

'What you waiting for?' Brian said, snapping her fingers at the distracted prince. 'We've got a half-fairy to find – there's no time to waste!'

Chapter Seven

*T*here were lots of things Cinders didn't especially enjoy. Doing the dishes, mopping the floors and clipping her stepmother's toenails on a Sunday evening were among her least favourite activities, but it turned out the thing she liked least of all was being trapped in a goblin's living room. Even though she felt as if

she'd been in there forever,
it had only been about
half an hour, but, in that
time, she'd already wished
up three big bags full of
gold.

'I'll be back when I've spent
all this,' the little man cackled as he waved on
his way out. 'Don't you go anywhere!'

Hilarious, Cinders thought, staring wistfully
at the door.

'He'd better let me have a go on
the FunStation,' she muttered,
stretching her legs out as far as
she could.

She looked round the

living room. Surely there had to be something she could do to get out of there even without magic. After all, she'd only been able to grant her own wishes for the last few days, and her dad always said she was a clever girl. She would get herself out of this pickle without wishing if she had to.

'There has to be at least one thing in here with his name on it,' she said out loud. 'If I can just find it, I can get out.'

Cinders's sisters had lots of things with their names on. Eleanor and Agnes had hats and T-shirts and jumpers and necklaces and badges and even special mugs that they took with them to the coffee shop in the village, all inscribed with their names. Cinders had written her name on the label of her nightie, but that was about it. Cinderella wasn't an especially popular name in the kingdom. Or anywhere else for that matter.

But there wasn't a single named necklace, special mug or even so much as a piece of post lying around the living room that displayed the goblin's name.

For the time being, at least, Cinders was stuck, but she wasn't ready to give up. She knew her friends were out there, probably searching high and low for her. Sparks, Hansel and Mouse would move mountains to find her, of that she was sure.

*

'Do you reckon Cinders will be mad that we've started without her?' Hansel asked Sparks, while stuffing his face with a particularly yummy

ham-and-cheese sandwich. This was his second particularly yummy ham-and-cheese sandwich of the ten particularly yummy ham-and-cheese sandwiches they had bought with their magic gold. While Cinders was trapped in the goblin's front room, Sparks and Hansel were halfway through a most delicious picnic.

The big red dog looked at the boy with a very serious expression on his face.

'Cinders never needs to know,' he instructed. 'Besides, if she was that hungry, she wouldn't have run off and disappeared, would she?'

They had returned to the spot where they'd left her very promptly, but she wasn't there. Well, it was fairly promptly . . . After they'd both gone for a wee, washed their hands, had a drink of pop and a hot dog, wandered around a bit, then been to find the sandwich stand. It wasn't their fault. There really was an awful lot to see at a marketplace halfway to Fairyland.

'Sparks, have you always known that Cinders's mum was a fairy?' Hansel asked.

'I can't remember everything from when I was a puppy,' Sparks replied. 'But I always knew she was special.'

'Did you know Cinders was a fairy?' Hansel asked.

'I got an idea about it when she wished me a metre up off the ground,' Sparks replied, growling at the memory. Dogs were not meant to fly.

'Do you think Cinders likes me?' Hansel asked.

'You're full of questions today,' Sparks said, snaffling another sausage. 'What's brought on this sudden and uncharacteristic quest for knowledge?'

Two pink spots blossomed in Hansel's cheeks.

'Just wondering is all,' he mumbled as he took another bite of his sandwich. 'Sometimes I'm not sure.'

'Perhaps a better question would be: do you like Cinders?' Sparks asked.

Colouring up, Hansel brushed the crumbs off
his face and straightened his little hat.

'On to more important things – how much
money have we got left?'

'More than enough,' Sparks replied, pawing
through their stash of coins. 'I think we should
look for some dessert. Wherever Cinders has
disappeared to, I'm sure she'll come running
back at the first sniff of a freshly baked
doughnut.'

Hansel gave a confirming nod and the two
of them set off into the market once again,
weaving in and out of the stalls, following their
noses with happy hearts.

'You like Cinders, don't you?' Sparks asked,
trotting alongside Hansel.

'For a half-fairy, half-girl who can do magic and almost got us eaten by a munklepoop,' Hansel said, blushing so brightly that even the tips of his ears turned bright red, 'she's all right.'

Sparks grinned, his tail wagging extra hard.

'Say, isn't that Mouse?' Hansel asked, pointing across the marketplace.

'Don't you try to change the subject,' Sparks woofed. 'You admitted it! You like Cinders!'

'No, really!' Hansel yelled as a tall speckled horse with big, flickering whiskers careened around the market, crashing into stalls, dodging the angry stallholders and squeaking in a loud and very un-horse-like manner. 'It's definitely Mouse, and Cinders isn't with him!'

'Wherever has she got to?' Sparks wondered,

his fur bristling with worry. It wouldn't be the first time Cinders had found herself in deep trouble, after all.

'Mouse!' cried Hansel, leaping into his path. 'Mouse, stop! It's us! Where's Cinders?'

But, if Mouse recognised them, he didn't show it. His eyes were wild and his whiskers were twitching and he looked very, very worried indeed.

'Grab that mouse-horse!' Sparks barked as Mouse raced towards them, galloping faster than ever. Hansel readied himself, arms outstretched, legs bent, ready to grab Mouse's reins as he ran by. Mouse came closer, Hansel squatted lower, reached out, grasped the reins and—

'Whoa there!' he yelped as Mouse kept on galloping, Hansel still clinging to the reins. 'Sparks! Help!'

'A dog's work is never done,' groaned the shaggy red dog as he took off after the runaway Mouse and the boy that was being dragged along beside him.

Chapter Eight

Most people would think it would be hard to sneak out of a palace and creep off to meet a witch to buy a magical potion when the king, who lived in the castle, hated witches and magic, but it was really quite easy.

Or at least it was easy if you were as good at sneaking around as Margery.

The witch in question was the same witch

who lived in a lovely gingerbread cottage, not far from Hansel's house, and her name was Veronica. She knew lots of people liked to tell stories about witches, about how they're mean and they wear black all the time and they're forever cooking children, but, other than enjoying a very stylish black ensemble from time to time, Veronica wasn't anything like those kinds of witches. For starters, she was a vegan.

'Knock-knock!' Margery called as she opened the door to the witch's cottage and let herself in. They had known each other for years, but you

wouldn't exactly call them friends. Mostly
because Margery didn't really have any friends.

'Hello,' Veronica replied, waving to Cinders's
stepmother from behind her
cauldron where she was stirring
up something that smelled
delicious, like caramel and
cocoa and the first bite of a
birthday cake. 'What can I
do for you today?'

Veronica was not
entirely thrilled to see
Margery in her home. She
only came to visit when she
wanted something.

'It's my poor, dear husband,'

Margery said, swooning on to the settee in the middle of the living room. Very comfy, she noted, wondering whether or not she should buy the same one for her new, soon-to-be-permanent quarters at the palace. 'I'm sure you've heard the news?'

Veronica nodded. She had heard the news, but she was having trouble believing it. She'd known Cinders ever since she was a little girl and yes, she'd been known to get into the occasional scrape now and then but, for the most part, she was an outstanding girl. Always kind and polite and ready to help out, and very often carrying snacks. The thought that she might have been running round the kingdom, casting evil spells on people, seemed

very unlikely to Veronica. While she preferred the term 'herbal mixologist' to 'witch', she did have an idea of how hard it was to cast spells, especially evil ones. Cinders didn't have the heart for it.

'Do you want me to see if I can bring Cinders home?'

'Cripes, no!' Margery frowned. 'I need more of your sleeping draught, for her father. He's been in a terrible state ever since she ran away, and it's the only thing that helps him get any rest.'

Veronica raised one perfectly groomed eyebrow. She was a very well turned-out woman.

'You need more?' she asked cautiously. 'But I

gave you a month's supply just last week. How much is he taking?'

Margery pursed her lips. She needed to play this one carefully. As far as anyone else was concerned, Cinders's father had fallen into a deep sleep ever since his daughter went missing. No one needed to know she had been slipping him a sleeping potion to keep him that way.

'I'm following your instructions to the letter,' she replied in a haughty tone. 'Although, I must confess, I might have taken a smidgen myself.'

But Veronica still didn't look convinced.

'And maybe my girls have popped a drop or two into their bedtime hot chocolate,' Margery added.

'Even so,' Veronica said, 'you've got through it awfully quickly, Margery. One spoonful of

that potion is enough to put an elephant to sleep for a year.'

Margery sat up on the sofa and fixed her sort-of friend with a very stern glare.

'It's a very nice home you've got here,' she said, standing up and walking round the room, taking in all of Veronica's lovely things. 'You have heard the king is cracking down on all things magical, I suppose? It would be such a shame if he sent a search party here. They're not terribly careful with people's belongings.'

Veronica set down her ladle, the cauldron bubbling before her.

'And breaking your things is probably the best-case scenario,' Margery went on, picking up a particularly pretty vase. 'I'd absolutely,

positively hate it if they ended up throwing you in the dungeons.'

'And why would the king send a search party here?' Veronica asked quietly. 'Is that a threat?'

The other woman turned round with a big smile on her face.

'Yes,' she said, sounding utterly relieved. 'I'm so glad you caught on. I was worried I was being too subtle. Now, about the sleeping draught?'

With great reluctance, Veronica pulled a large blue glass bottle from the shelf behind her and handed it over.

'Be very careful with it,' she warned. 'If you

take too much, there's a very good chance you'll never wake up.'

Margery's eyes glittered with happiness.

'Is that so?' she replied, smiling so broadly that Veronica could see all her teeth. 'That's very helpful to know.'

With one last dashing grin, she turned on her heel and walked towards the door.

'Say,' she called over her shoulder, one hand on the door handle. 'Where did you get your settee?'

'It's one of a kind,' Veronica replied. 'Custom-made.'

'Hmm,' Margery said as she let herself out. 'That's a shame, isn't it?'

The witch couldn't quite work out whether

it was a shame for her or a shame for Margery,
but, either way, she was very, very worried.

'Lovely to see you!' Margery sang. 'We must
do this again soon . . . if you're still here.'

And

then

she

was

gone.

Chapter Nine

'So, my dad said there haven't been any fairies in the kingdom for more than a hundred years,' Joderick said, traipsing behind Brian as they scoured the marketplace. At each and every stall, Joderick was supposed to distract the stall owner while Brian searched for Cinders. So far they hadn't found anything other than some interesting pyramid-shaped

soaps, a pair of cufflinks made out of stardust and a strong telling-off from a man selling feelings.

'A hundred years?' Brian asked. 'Well, that's tosh, isn't it?'

'I don't know,' Joderick replied, struggling to keep up with her. 'Is it?'

'Cinders has been there in the last hundred years. Her mum was there in the last hundred years. I was there last week. I'm not sure your dad knows what he's on about, you sweet idiot.'

Joderick beamed at the insult. He was so used to everyone sucking up to him all the time, it was quite a refreshing change to have someone call him an idiot. Not very nice perhaps, but for Joderick it was different.

'I suspect he might be keeping secrets from me,' Joderick admitted. 'But I don't think my dad would tell lies.'

Brian marched on, shaking her head.

'Lots of people do things they know they shouldn't because someone they trust told them to,' she said. 'Before you met Cinders, did you think all fairies were evil?'

Joderick thought about this for a moment. 'Yes,' he admitted. 'I did.'

'And why did you think that?'

'Because everyone says they are,' Joderick reasoned.

'And there you go,' Brian replied, pausing to look underneath a golden violin stall. 'What if everyone told your dad fairies were evil and that

they hadn't been in the kingdom for a hundred years? If he believed them and didn't try to find out for himself, he wouldn't know he was telling lies, would he?'

Joderick marched behind her with a furrowed brow. It was a lot to think about.

'I found a map hidden in his desk, along with a painting of a lady,' he told Brian, casting his eyes back and forth at all the magical, marvellous things for sale in the market. Glove puppets that could talk for themselves, strap-on wings that actually flew, a book that read itself out loud. He was finding it harder and harder to understand why his father and his grandfather had been so determined to keep magic out of their kingdom.

'I don't think he wanted me to find them,' Joderick said.

'I should say he didn't,' Brian agreed. 'Most people don't hide things they want other

Hello!

Woof!

people to find, especially maps, and especially, especially paintings of ladies.'

'And I think there could be other things he's hiding from me,' Joderick added.

'And I think you're not as green as you are cabbage-looking,' Brian said with a smile that faded quickly from her face. 'Oh, doodleflip, there's that pesky goblin again.'

The prince looked round quickly to see the short man, this time wearing an even bigger and fancier hat than before.

'That's an awfully big bag of gold he's carrying,' he said, noticing a few stray coins spilling out of the top of the sack he carried over his shoulder. 'Are all goblins as rich as him?'

98

'No,' Brian replied, squinting at the goblin to get a better look. 'And, the last time I checked, he wasn't remotely rich either. Something's going on here.'

Joderick's newly neon-green eyes lit up with excitement.

'Shall we follow him?' he suggested.

'I think I know where he's going,' Brian said with a sigh. 'But let's keep our distance. I really don't want to speak to him unless I have to. Honestly, he loves talking about himself and I don't have the patience for it today.'

The prince nodded and followed close behind his new fairy friend with his skin blue, his hair silver and gold and his identity hidden in plain sight.

Chapter Ten

'Where are you taking us?' Hansel wailed as Mouse finally slowed down to a trot. Sparks bounded up alongside the duo, panting heavily, which did not please him in the slightest. Sparks was not a dog who liked getting out of breath. Eventually, Mouse stopped altogether and Hansel let go of his reins. Who would have thought a horse that

used to be a mouse could run so fast?

They were out of the market now, he realised, surrounded by small, peculiar-looking houses with doors and windows so tiny that Hansel had to crouch down to look inside.

'Is Cinders in one of these houses, Mouse?'

Sparks asked, sniffing the air and trying to get a whiff of his best friend. Mouse squeaked wildly, pointing a hoof down a dark alleyway and flicking his long pink tail with impatience.

'I'll go,' the dog offered, although it was more that he didn't trust Hansel to get the job done than because he was feeling especially brave.

Slowly, he padded down the alleyway, keeping as low to the ground as he could. At the end was a small wooden door, half the height of the door to their cottage at home, perhaps even a little smaller than that.

'Cinders?' he growled softly. 'Can you hear me?'

'Sparks?' a voice piped up from behind the door. 'Is that you?'

'Cinders!' the dog yelped with joy as a pair of eyes he would recognise anywhere peeped at him through the letterbox. 'It is you!'

Truly, Cinders could not think of a time she had been happier to see her doggy pal.

'I knew you'd find me,' she said, wiping away a little tear of happiness. 'I knew you'd be hunting high and low.'

'Um, yes,' Sparks replied with a woof. 'That's exactly what we were doing, definitely not eating sandwiches and hot dogs in the marketplace. Now, open up and let us in.'

'Bit of a problem there,' Cinders sighed and tried to poke her finger through the letterbox. 'I'm trapped in here! I followed a goblin home and now he's cast a spell on the house so I can

never leave. He wants me to stay here and wish up piles of gold for him forever.'

Sparks barked with incredulity. 'What on earth were you doing following a goblin back to his house?' he asked. 'You know better than to follow strangers.'

'He said he had a restaurant and that you were there already,' she replied, somewhat embarrassed. 'He said he had sausages.'

Sparks gave a sage, doggy nod. 'Well, in that case, I completely understand.'

But, understand as he might, he had no idea how to get Cinders out of the enchanted house. He pulled on the door, rattled the letterbox and even tried to climb in through the window. But nothing worked.

'Make way for Hansel!'

Cinders and Sparks looked up to see Hansel charging down the alleyway at full speed.

'I'll break down the door if I have to!' he bellowed. 'Move out of the way, Sparks – I'm coming through!'

'Oh, no,' Cinders groaned. She covered her eyes with her fingers and then peeked between them just a tiny bit.

Before anyone could try to stop him, Hansel leaped into the air with a triumphant cry – and bashed right into the little wooden door.

It did not budge.

'That was a very good try, but the only way for anyone to get in or out of the house is to say the goblin's name out loud,' Cinders explained, and Hansel rolled over on the ground, looking really quite sheepish. 'But I've no idea what it is.'

'Could it be John?' Sparks asked. 'I feel like there are a lot of Johns in the world. Or have you tried Nicholas? Good solid name is Nicholas.'

'I reckon it's Jeff,' Hansel offered, rubbing his foot. The door was much harder than

he had anticipated. 'Or Jimmy.'

Cinders was trying very hard not to get annoyed, but the goblin could be back any minute and, if he found Sparks, Hansel and Mouse outside his house, they were going to end up trapped right alongside her, and every minute she spent trapped in this house, she was most definitely not on her way to Fairyland.

'I know, why don't we split up and look for the goblin?' Sparks suggested, seeing a very familiar look on Cinders's face. 'Me and Mouse can go back to the market, Hansel can hang out around here and, when we find the goblin, we'll just ask him his name. Then we all come back here and – bingo bongo! – you're free.'

'That's a very good idea,' Cinders said,

clapping with joy. She really was so happy to see her friends. For a split second, she'd begun to worry that no one would find her, that she'd never see Sparks or Hansel or Mouse or her family ever again, and that she would never complete her quest to Fairyland. It had not been fun, even for a split second.

'What does he look like?' Hansel asked her. 'Tall? Short?'

'He's a goblin,' she said. 'So he's short . . . like a goblin.'

'Handsome?' Sparks asked. 'Or not so much?'

'I don't think goblins are renowned for their good looks,' Cinders answered. 'He's a goblin; he looks like a goblin. Little, long grey beard, very big, pointy hat.'

'Sounds pretty cool to me.' Hansel sniffed.

Cinders closed the letterbox for a moment and rolled her eyes.

'Shall we get this mission started?' she said through the door. 'He'll be back any minute.'

'We'll find him, Cinders, I promise!' Sparks shouted as he raced away with Mouse. 'I'll be back faster than you can say sausages.'

'Sausages,' she whispered, watching them go.

Hansel got to his knees, still quite sore from trying to break down the door, but mostly worried about his friend. 'It'll be all right,' he whispered back. 'I promise.'

'What will be all right?' asked a voice behind him.

Very slowly, Hansel turned round to see a

short man with a long grey beard and a very big, pointy hat that he immediately thought looked very cool. The goblin!

'Um, the price of milk,' Hansel replied, thinking as fast as he could. 'I was just explaining to the young lady of the house that my farm can deliver all your daily dairy needs for half the cost of whatever you're paying your current milkman.'

Cinders held her breath. Would the goblin believe him?

'Half-price milk, you say?' the goblin replied. 'What about yoghurts? I love yoghurts.'

'Oh, yes,' Hansel said. 'Those too. All I need to get you set up is your name, address and phone number. But most important is

your name – definitely need that.'

'Hmm.' The goblin stroked his beard as he considered Hansel's story. 'Why don't I write it down for you? Do come inside.'

'Hansel, no!' Cinders yelled, but it was too late. The goblin had already opened the door and shoved poor Hansel inside. Now he was trapped in the enchanted house alongside his friend.

'I don't suppose you've got any magical powers, have you?' the goblin asked, looking the boy up and down. Cinders reached out to grab Hansel's hand and gave it a squeeze.

Hansel shook his head, feeling somewhat frightened and very foolish. 'I don't think so.'

'In that case, I might call my friend Frank the Bear and see if he's feeling peckish. Always going on about eating pesky kids is Frank,' the goblin said before grabbing Cinders's latest load of wished-up gold. 'I want ten more bags before I get back!'

And, with that, he

was

gone.

Chapter Eleven

As soon as Margery arrived back at the
palace, she made her way straight to her
husband's bedchamber. As far as anyone knew,
Cinders's father, the king's favourite builder,
had been terribly ill ever since they'd arrived
at the palace, hardly even opening his eyes.
The king reckoned he was faking it to avoid
answering some difficult questions about his

wayward daughter. The queen thought a nice long nap sounded very appealing. But Margery was the only one who really knew the truth . . .

'Time to wake up, dear,' she said, settling down at her husband's side and gently shaking him awake.

He rubbed his eyes and blinked. The room was very dark and very small compared to Margery's. In fact, it was the smallest and darkest room in the palace and also the furthest away from the king and queen. Margery had insisted it was the best place for her husband to recover, and no one dared argue with Margery.

'Is that you, Cinders?' he asked weakly.

'No, no,' she replied. 'That little madam is still missing. How do you feel?'

'I'm fine,' insisted the old man as he attempted to sit up straight. 'Just a little tired. Perhaps you could open the curtains and let some light in? I have to go out and find Cinders. There's something she needs to know.'

'Yes, yes, all in good time,' Margery said, popping the cork on the witch's sleeping potion and pouring it into the cup at the side of her husband's bed. 'Are you thirsty? I've brought you something delicious to drink . . .'

She held the cup up to his

lips and tipped it back until he had drunk every
last drop.

'Have you heard from Prince Joderick?' he
asked. 'I do worry about him out there with all
those munklepoops and gadzoozles.'

'Not to mention the fairies,' Margery added,
a very worried look on her face. If there was
one thing they could agree on, it was that they
both wanted Prince Joderick home as soon as
possible. Even if they wanted him home for
slightly different reasons.

'We needn't worry about the fairies,' Cinders's
father muttered. 'The fairies are good. The
fairies won't hurt their own.'

Margery looked confused. 'But Prince
Joderick isn't a fairy.'

Her husband shook his head, his eyes already drooping from the effects of the sleeping potion.

'Not Joderick,' he whispered. 'Cinders . . .'

And then his eyes closed and he drifted off to sleep.

*

Sparks had looked everywhere for the goblin. He'd looked high, he'd looked low, he'd looked far and he'd looked wide, but he hadn't been able to spot that short man with the long grey beard and big, tall hat anywhere.

'Maybe we should go back to the house,' he said to Mouse who nodded in agreement. 'Perhaps Hansel or Cinders have discovered his name by now and are ready to leave for Fairyland.'

This time Mouse didn't look quite so sure.

True, he was only a horse who used to be a mouse, but he wasn't stupid. Hansel was a nice boy, but Mouse couldn't quite see him tricking a very cunning goblin into telling him his name.

Mouse didn't know how right he was.

The sun was already starting to dip behind the mountain and the last thing Sparks wanted was to be stuck in this market after dark. Who knew what shenanigans went on here at night-time? And he couldn't leave Cinders alone with the goblin in that house. Even if he had to sit outside the front door all night long, that's what he would do.

The big red talking dog and the horse that used to be a mouse were just about to turn round and head back the way they came when what did they see coming round the corner but a short

man with a long grey beard and a very, very tall, pointed hat.

'Mouse!' Sparks gasped. 'Do you think that's him?'

Mouse squeaked back and rolled his eyes.

'Let's follow him,' Sparks suggested. 'If we can learn his name and give it to Cinders, we'll find out one way or another.'

Mouse snuffled his nose and wiggled his whiskers. It was as good a plan as any.

Slowly, they crept after the goblin, stopping when he stopped, turning when he turned. They followed him through the market, over a bridge and all the way to the other side of the town, right to the foot of the mountain until they came to a building that had no windows, and

a door at the front. Above the door was a sign that said CROONERS. The goblin stopped outside, took off his hat, smoothed down his hair and said hello to the rather large bear that was standing in front of the door. The goblin gave him a gold coin, popped his hat back on and went inside.

'Well, I'll be a giddy aunt,' Sparks muttered. 'He's going to do karaoke.'

It's a little known fact that goblins love karaoke, and it was this particular goblin's favourite thing in the whole wide world. He'd had a very good day, he reasoned as he hopped up on a stool inside Crooners and ordered himself a pumpkin juice. He'd captured a magical halfling, got himself a new FunStation and an excellent hat. It was definitely time to

unwind with a tune or two.

Outside the karaoke bar, Sparks was at a bit of a loss. How were they supposed to sneak past the bear?

'If we can get in, we'll definitely be able to find out the goblin's name,' he told Mouse, his bushy red tail swishing back and forth while he concentrated. 'But I don't have any gold left to pay the bear on the door – Hansel has it all. What are we going to do? Perhaps, if I talk to him, I can explain what's happening and he'll help us out. Or maybe there's a back entrance I can creep through? Or we could dress up as health inspectors that have come to check how clean the place is.'

Or, thought Mouse, *I could knock over*

all these rubbish bins and run away.

Since Sparks couldn't read his mind,
Mouse decided his plan was just as
good as any and trotted over to
the bins, crouched down on his
front legs and kicked as hard as
he could with his back legs.

'Oi!' the bear
shouted. 'What
do you think
you're doing?'

Mouse winked
at Sparks and kicked again,
sending the bins and the rubbish flying
all over the place.

'You are so gonna get a knuckle sandwich!'

the bear shouted, stepping towards Mouse. But, before he could so much as raise a paw, Mouse was off like a shot, running away down the street. And, just as he'd predicted, the bear chased after him.

'I hope he doesn't catch you, Mouse!' Sparks gasped as he bounded into Crooners just in time to see a lady goblin wearing a very sparkly purple dress and holding a microphone take the stage.

'Next up we have one of our regulars,' she announced. 'Everyone put your hands together for . . .

RUMPELSTILTSKIN!'

Sparks gasped as the little man in the tall
hat hopped off his stool and climbed up on
to the stage.

The goblin was just about to open his
mouth and begin his song when he saw a very
bushy red tail swoosh out of the front door
and disappear. It was the dog he'd seen with
Cinders!

'Blummin' blumkins!' he growled, tossing
the microphone back to the lady in
the purple dress and leaping from
the stage. He had to catch that
dog. There was no way he
was going to lose his little
goldmine!

Chapter Twelve

Sparks had never run as fast in his entire life. Not when Margery had caught him stealing sausages from the fridge, not when Agnes started her violin lessons and not even when Cinders hung her stinky socks right over his doggy bed.

Mouse had quickly outrun the bear. He was much faster and much stronger and much more

used to darting around in tight spaces, what
with having spent most of his life as a rodent,
and, by the time Sparks made it back to the
bridge, Mouse was right by his side.

'I know his name!' he barked with joy. 'We
can free Cinders and continue on our way!'

Mouse squeaked with joy as they galloped on.

'Get on outta here!' the bear shouted, shaking
his fist as the friends ran off. 'You're barred, the
pair of you!'

*

By the time they got back to the goblin's house,
Mouse and Sparks were both so out of breath,
they couldn't even knock on the door.

'Sparks, is that you?' Cinders called, hearing a
commotion outside.

'I heard hooves!' Hansel added. 'Is it Mouse?'

'Why are you inside the house?' Sparks puffed, realising there were two pairs of eyes peering at him through the letterbox. 'You were supposed to be rescuing Cinders, not keeping her company.'

'We are aware that was the original plan,' Cinders grumbled as Hansel blushed, embarrassed. 'What are you doing back here? Did you find out the goblin's name?'

'We most certainly did,' Sparks said, puffing out his chest with pride. 'You'll never guess what it is . . .'

'No! We won't!' she shouted. 'That's sort of the whole point, Sparks. What are you waiting for?'

To be fair, she had been trapped in the house
all day and was very, very impatient to get out.

'Calm down, calm down,' he said gruffly.
'I'm getting to that. His name is—'

'Don't you dare!' screeched the goblin,
tearing round the corner on a little
electric scooter. It was amazing what
you could get your hands on
when you had bags
and bags of
ill-gotten
gold.

'Don't you say it!' he bawled as he launched himself from the scooter on to Sparks's back, trying desperately to wrap his arms round his muzzle. Sparks kicked and barked and bucked and howled, but the goblin was much stronger than he looked and refused to let go.

'If you keep quiet,' he bargained, hanging on for dear life as Sparks attempted to toss him off his back, 'I'll give you everything you ever wanted.'

'All I want is you off my back!' the dog barked, running round and round and round in mad circles until the goblin flew through the air and landed –

PLOP! – right in front of his own front door.

'Your name is Rumpelstiltskin!' Sparks shouted. 'Now open the door and let Cinders and Hansel go free!'

The goblin looked at Sparks, he looked at Mouse, he looked at Hansel and he looked at Cinders. And then he laughed.

'What's so funny?' Cinders asked, yanking the door handle with all her might. It didn't even start to budge. 'You said you'd let me go if I learned your name. Well, I've learned it and now you have to let me out.'

'Yes, I do remember saying that,' Rumpelstiltskin replied. 'But I also remember trapping you in my house and making you wish up piles of gold. Do those sound like the actions of a goblin who is planning to keep his promises?'

Cinders gasped. Everyone knew that there was nothing in the world worse than breaking a promise.

'Letting you go would be silly,' the goblin went on, before dropping to the ground and busting out a pretty good breakdancing routine. 'So you can go around shouting my name as much as you like, but I'm not going to let you go. I'm Rumpelstiltskin and I'm the cleverest goblin that ever there was.'

'I think we both know that isn't true, Rumpy.'

Cinders peeped past the dancing goblin, squinting to see just who was talking. Short, red-haired, sparkly wings . . . it couldn't be.

'Cinderella? What are you doing in a goblin's house, you absolute plonker?'

Yes, it was definitely her.

'Brian!' Cinders cheered. 'I am so glad to see you!'

Chapter Thirteen

'*It really is you!*' *Cinders cried, accidentally* elbowing Hansel in the head in all the excitement. 'You've got to help us! This goblin tricked me into coming inside his house to wish up gold for him and said he would only let us out if we guessed his name, but we know his name and he still won't let us out.'

'Is that right?' Brian said, staring at the goblin

with her arms folded and a very stern look on her face.

'Long time no see,' Rumpelstiltskin said, combing down his eyebrows and winking at the fairy. 'Nice to see you, Brian.'

'Wish I could say the same,' she replied. 'I see you've been up to your old tricks again? Lying to fairies and breaking your word.'

'I don't know what you mean,' he said, edging

in front of the door to block Cinders's view.
'I didn't trick them – they came inside of their
own accord.'

'And now you're going to let them out of
your own accord.' Brian spoke with a warning
in her voice. 'Unless you'd like to explain
yourself to the king and queen of Fairyland.'

'Ooh, I say,' Hansel muttered.

'I know, right?' Cinders agreed with an
impressed whistle. 'My fairy godmother is the
best.'

The goblin began to turn red. He knew when
he was beaten, but it didn't mean he had to be
happy about it. He stamped his foot and shook
his head.

'No!' he shouted. 'I'm not going to let them

out. I still haven't bought all the things I want. She's not going anywhere!'

Brian fluttered her wings and sighed. He always had been a giant pain in the bum.

'Fine,' she said through gritted teeth. 'I'll let them out myself. Zimzamzoom!'

A shower of silver sparks shot from Brian's fingers and lit up the goblin's entire house.

'Go and open the door, Noderick,' she ordered as Rumpelstiltskin stood and watched with his mouth hanging open in shock.

'Noderick?' Cinders gasped as a blue-skinned boy with gold and silver hair walked carefully past the sulking goblin and opened the door. 'Jodders, is that you?'

'It most certainly is,' he replied. 'Prince Joderick Jorenson Picklebottom at your service.'

'I still prefer Noderick,' Brian muttered to Mouse who nodded in agreement as Cinders rushed at her friend and gave him the biggest hug he'd ever received in his life.

'Jodders!' Cinders cried as Brian's spell disappeared, returning Joderick to his normal

(and slightly more boring now that he came to think about it) colours. 'What on earth are you doing here?'

'I came to get my trousers back,' he said, nodding at Cinders's outfit. She laughed and stuck her hands in the pockets. *Quite funny*, she thought, but he wasn't having them. They were the best pair of trousers she'd ever worn in her life.

'Enjoy yourselves while you can,' Rumpelstiltskin said, still stamping his feet in a strop. 'But I called the palace earlier today and they're sending someone with the reward. One hundred gold pieces all for me!'

Sparks barked in disgust. 'Magic gold wasn't enough for you?'

'This is what happens when you're greedy,' Brian said. 'It turns you bitter and mean. Nothing is ever enough.'

'Doesn't matter what you think,' the goblin said with a gleeful laugh. 'I spoke to a very lovely lady called Margery and she said she would send someone out to see me right away. I should imagine they'll be here any minute.'

'Margery?' Cinders asked with a gulp. 'You're sure you spoke to someone called Margery?'

'Oh, yes,' he confirmed. 'I wrote it down so I'd know who to complain about if the money didn't show up.'

'Classic Rumpy,' groaned Brian. 'All right, everyone, I think we should get out of here. I'll deal with him later. If the palace knows where you are, there's every chance they've sent a very specific someone to find you.'

'My dad?' Cinders said hopefully.

Joderick shook his head.

'My stepmother?' she asked, considerably less hopeful.

'I'm afraid not.' Joderick gulped. 'My dad was so mad when I came to find you, he sent . . .'

But, before he could finish his sentence, a BIG, booming voice interrupted.

'HE SENT ME.'

Chapter Fourteen

*E*veryone turned as one to see a tall man with a thick beard, mounted on a huge black steed. He was dressed head to toe in black, and a very shiny silver axe hung from his belt.

That's a very impressive beard, thought Rumpelstiltskin.

That's a very scary axe, thought Hansel.

That's a very good-looking horse, thought Mouse, batting his eyelids at the other horse.

'Prince Joderick and Cinders,' the Huntsman boomed. 'You are to come with me, by order of the king.'

Cinders, finally free of the goblin's house, felt her fingers tingle with magic.

'What if we don't want to go with you?' she asked fiercely.

'If it's quite all right with you, I'm going to pop back inside,' Rumpelstiltskin said. 'I think I've left the hob on.'

'No, you haven't,' Hansel said.

'No,' he agreed, running inside and slamming the door. 'I haven't.'

'You will both come with me of your own free will or I'll take you against it,' the Huntsman replied, one hand on his axe. It seemed to Cinders that he was really rather hoping that they'd refuse to do things the easy way.

'I've got a plan,' Hansel whispered to Cinders. 'Do you trust me?'

She nodded right away.

'Okay, then, just do as I say,' he said before

walking up to the Huntsman,
as brave as brave could be.

'My friends won't be coming
with you today,' he said in a
wibbly-wobbly voice.

'Is that so?' replied the man in
black. 'And why is that?'

'Because they're going to
run!' Hansel yelled. All at
once, he, Cinders, Joderick,
Sparks and Mouse all
scattered in different directions,
leaving the Huntsman and

Brian standing in front of the goblin's house. The Huntsman looked very annoyed, but Brian couldn't stop laughing.

'You've got to give it to the kid,' she said, pressing her hand into her side. She'd laughed so hard, she'd given herself a stitch again. 'He certainly fooled you there.'

'He didn't fool me!' the Huntsman growled. 'I'll have them all rounded up in no time at all.'

With an angry flourish, he spun round on his horse and set off after his prey.

'Oh,' Brian sighed,

wiping away a happy tear. 'It does the heart good to have a giggle sometimes. But I suppose I'd better help them.'

Everyone was running as fast they could, coming together as they reached the marketplace where the stallholders were packing up for the day.

'What shall we do now?' yelled Hansel.

'Where shall we go?' wailed Joderick.

'Has anyone got any sausages?' shrieked Sparks.

But Cinders stayed quiet. *There was no way they could outrun the Huntsman forever, and there was no way he was going to let them go without a fight. He was just so scary. If only they could scare him somehow.*

'I thought you'd never ask,' Brian said,

suddenly appearing at her side. 'I know how to scare him.'

'Did you just read my mind?' Cinders gasped.

'Don't look so surprised – you were practically shouting,' Brian grumbled before leaning in and whispering in her goddaughter's ear. 'Got it?'

'Got it,' Cinders confirmed with a grin before pulling a cookie out of her pocket. 'Mouse, come here!'

'Did you have that in your pocket the entire time we were in the goblin's house?' asked Hansel with wide eyes. 'You knew I was starving!'

'She really is a mind-reader!' Joderick gasped, staring at Brian in admiration.

'Now is not the time for a discussion about food,' Cinders cried as she took a big bite of the

cookie, chewing quickly. 'Quick, here he comes!'

As the Huntsman galloped closer and closer and closer, Cinders climbed on Mouse's back and whispered something to her friend. He squeaked in agreement and Cinders sat up with a smile on her face.

'Gotcha!'

The Huntsman swooped by and scooped her up off Mouse's back, but Cinders didn't struggle at all. Instead she closed her eyes and shouted out: 'I wish Mouse was a mouse again!'

Her fingers tingled and sparkled, and gold and silver glitter shot out all around her. The Huntsman's horse stopped dead in its tracks as the odd-looking horse that had given it a wink began to sparkle in just the same way.

'What are you doing?' yelled the Huntsman. 'Keep going!'

But his horse just stamped its hooves and snorted, tracking backwards away from the glittering horse as it sparkled and shimmered and then – **POP!** – it turned into a little speckled mouse.

'A MOUSE!' shrieked the Huntsman as his horse reared up on its hindquarters. The big, burly man was so afraid of the little, squeaky mouse that he let go of Cinders, who floated to the floor and landed on her feet.

'Well, I'll be,' muttered Sparks, more impressed at Cinders's graceful landing than the big, burly Huntsman being afraid of a tiny little mouse.

'Get it away from me!' the fearless Huntsman squealed, covering his eyes with his hands. 'I hate mice!'

'That's our cue to leave,' Brian said, appearing beside the group and snapping her fingers. 'Bye, Hunty!'

And then Cinders and Sparks and Mouse and Hansel and Prince Joderick Jorenson Picklebottom all disappeared

in a puff of

smoke.

Chapter Fifteen

'Where are we?' asked Cinders, wrapping her arms round herself. She was shivering from head to toe. Wherever Brian had wished them away to was very, very cold. There was even snow on the ground and, the last time Cinders had checked, it was practically spring.

'We're on the mountain pass,' Brian replied. 'And, if anyone asks, no, I most certainly did

not magic any of you through a shortcut.'

Cinders smiled gratefully, even if her teeth were chattering the whole time.

'This part of your journey isn't going to be easy,' Brian warned as she produced three very big, thick jumpers from her tiny little handbag and handed them out to Cinders, Hansel and Jodders. 'The mountain pass can be very treacherous and, if you thought munklepoops were bad, wait until you get a load of a klankinsaur.'

'Are you sure you couldn't magic us a little bit further along?' asked Sparks as Cinders yanked a perfectly sized doggy jumper over his head.

'Quite sure,' Brian replied crisply.

Hansel looked at Joderick's red jumper and Joderick looked at Hansel's blue jumper and the two happily swapped with friendly smiles.

'Before I forget, I found something in my dad's desk that I wanted to show you,' Joderick said to Cinders, digging around in his pocket and pulling out the square of silk that held the very old painting. 'Don't you think it looks like you?'

'Good golly gosh!' Cinders breathed. 'It really does. If my hair was neater and my nose was smaller, this could be a painting of me!'

'I should think it does look like you,' Brian said, peering over Joderick's shoulder to take a closer look. 'That's a painting of your mother.'

Everyone – Hansel, Joderick, Sparks, Cinders and even the tiny mouse, Mouse – gasped.

'That's my mum?' Cinders asked, staring at the smiling girl in the painting. 'But why would the king have a painting of my mum?'

Brian did not reply straight away. She knew she had already said too much. The deal was that she could guide her goddaughter and help her when she was in need, but she couldn't tell her exactly what had happened. That would break her promise, which would break the truce, which would result in something very bad indeed. Cinders would just have to figure this one out for herself.

'Perhaps he collects paintings?' she said with a shrug. 'If I were you, I'd put that away. Doesn't look like it would take more than a few snowflakes to ruin it and, judging by those storm clouds overhead, you're going to have to deal with more than a bit of snow before the night is out.'

Cinders nodded, but her heart sank as Jodders carefully wrapped the painting up and put it back in his pocket. All she wanted to do was curl up in a corner somewhere and stare at the painting. If only it could come to life and

answer her questions. She had so many.

'Very impressed with the wishing back there,' Sparks said, giving her a big old lovely lick. 'And the way you floated down from the horse? A plus, I should say.'

She smiled and gave her doggy pal a hug. 'Thanks, Sparks,' she whispered.

'Your magic is getting more advanced,' Brian agreed. 'The closer you get to Fairyland, the more powerful it will become. But don't go getting cocky. The more powerful you are, the more trouble you can find yourself in.'

'I'll be careful,' promised Cinders. 'Wait a minute, what do you mean the closer I get to Fairyland? You're not leaving again?'

Brian clapped her shoulder and set her face in

what she hoped passed for a supportive smile.

'I am,' she confirmed. 'But only because I have to. You'll be in Fairyland before you know it and I'll be there waiting for you. All of you.'

Brian took her hand from Cinders's shoulder and, for a moment, she felt even colder. But then a warm hand squeezed her other shoulder. It was Hansel.

'We'll get through this,' he told her. 'We've got this far, haven't we?'

'And I'm not going anywhere,' Joderick

added, placing his hand on her other shoulder. 'In fact, I'm quite excited about the adventure now that I'm certain the fairies aren't going to eat me.'

'I might give it a go if you don't stop being so cheesy,' Brain said, making a yucking sound that Sparks secretly sort of agreed with. 'Get on with you all – you want to travel as far as you can before dark. When the sun sets, find shelter right away. The last thing you need is to be out here when the bolves come out to hunt.'

'Bolves?' asked Cinders, not sure she really wanted any further explanation.

'Imagine a wolf crossed with a bear,' Brian replied. 'Without the sense of humour, but with a more dazzling fashion sense.'

'Fantastic,' said Joderick, puffing out his princely chest. 'I can't wait to see one.'

'Righto,' muttered Brian. 'Looks like the five of you can take care of yourselves.'

Without waiting for anyone to protest, she disappeared into thin air.

'The good thing is, we don't have to take care of ourselves,' Hansel said as Cinders scooped Mouse up out of the snow and slipped him safely inside her pocket.

She looked at her friend, a little bit confused. 'We don't?'

'We don't,' he confirmed.

'Because we can all take care of each other.'

'Last one to Fairyland is a rotten munklepoop!' cried Jodders, thrusting his arm into the air and running up the mountain pass, only to be overtaken by a very game Hansel, who whooped and laughed as he raced by.

'Maybe we could sneak back the other way and leave them to it,' Sparks suggested. 'I don't think they'd even notice if we weren't there.'

'I think it'll be best if we all stick together,' Cinders said with a very real smile on her face. 'The five of us on our way to Fairyland. What could possibly get in our way?'

Chapter Sixteen

'WHAT DO YOU MEAN THEY ESCAPED?'

The king was apoplectic.

'I say "escaped", but what I really mean is that they managed to temporarily get away from me,' the Huntsman replied, his head bowed, squatting down on one knee. He was feeling very awkward. He'd never had to explain why

he'd failed before, and he wasn't very good at it.

'And how exactly did they get away from you?' the king asked.

His eyes were very wide and his mouth was very small and, from where she was sitting, the queen could have sworn he was vibrating.

'Obviously they used great cunning and magnificent evil, and there were dozens of warriors with many weapons and also, possibly –' he looked down at his big black boots in shame – 'a mouse.'

'Be gone,' the king ordered. He couldn't even bear to look at him. 'Get out of my sight.'

'If you give me one more

chance, sire, I will return the prince to you post-haste,' the Huntsman promised.

'You're lucky I'm letting you keep your head,' King Poderick replied. 'Guards, take him to the dungeons. And make sure to fill his cell with cheese.'

'Noooooooo!'

Before the king's guards could act, the mighty Huntsman leaped to his feet and ran across the throne room.

'I refuse to surrender to those squeaky, cheese-eating monsters!' he bellowed.

And then he dived out of a window.

'Didn't see that coming,' the king muttered in surprise. 'Well, I suppose that's that.'

One of the pages dashed over to the window

to have a look. Down below, he saw the
Huntsman climbing out of the palace moat,
limping as he ran off into the Dark Forest.

'He's run off, Your Majesty,' he confirmed.
'Should we send someone after him?'

'Not unless you've got another Huntsman up
your sleeve,' the king grumbled. 'Now what are
we supposed to do?'

'You could always go after Joderick yourself?'
the queen suggested.

Everyone in the throne room held their breath.

'Uh, yes,' the king said, taking off his crown
and polishing it on the sleeve of his robe. 'I
could do that. That's something we should look
into. Advisers!'

At once, his team of trusted counsellors,

consultants and confidants crowded round him.

'Yes, Your Supreme Wonderfulness?' The first one to speak bowed low and deep.

'How may we assist you?' asked another.

'What do you think is the best way to get Joderick back to the palace and make sure this Cinders girl is gone for good?' he asked.

'I think, having taken all the options into account, such as the length of time he's been missing, the distance from the palace, the failure of the Huntsman, the little girl's magic powers, not to mention all this talk of mice . . .' The first adviser paused as all the others murmured in agreement. 'I think the best course of action would be to follow the queen's suggestion. You should go after Joderick.'

No one looked more surprised than the queen herself.

'Follow my suggestion?' she asked. 'Oh, I don't know if that's such a good idea. If only because it's quite possible that it has never actually been done before.'

'It's a very good idea,' said the second adviser, stroking his long beard.

'A strong suggestion,' agreed the first. 'The queen is very wise.'

'Oh, I say,' she said, blushing prettily. 'Get on with you.'

'While I would love to undertake the quest myself, I'm not certain I, the king, should leave the palace during these troubled times,' King Poderick said, pulling at the collar of his robes.

'Is anyone else hot in here? I'm very hot.'

The advisers all huddled together for a moment to discuss this hiccup before turning back to the king.

'We believe the people of the kingdom would be cheered to see their king go forth into the Dark Forest and bring back their beloved prince,' the first adviser declared. 'And also, no, we are not hot.'

'Then it's settled!' the queen called. 'My beloved husband, our brave and fearless king, will set out to save our son and bring him home this very eve!'

'This very eve?' the king asked as everyone began to cheer. 'Before dinner? Without a proper night's sleep?'

'My brave, heroic husband,' she said, lovingly stroking his cheek before gripping his arm very, very slightly. 'Bring my son home or I'll blimmin' well throw you out of the window after that Huntsman.'

*

Everyone in the palace – and soon the entire kingdom – was celebrating the king's pledge to go forth and find Prince Joderick himself. Everyone, that is, except for Margery.

'That king is as useful as a chocolate teapot!' she yelled, slamming the door to her bedchamber and rifling through a secret locked cupboard for which she had the only key. 'There's just one way we'll get the prince back to the castle and that's if someone gets

Cinders out of the way first.'

She pulled out a shiny red apple, the big blue
bottle of sleeping potion and a long black cloak,
smiling as she laid them all out on her settee.
The settee that used to live in Veronica the
witch's house . . . Margery
turned to smile at
herself in the mirror.

'And that
someone,' she
said, 'is going
to be me.'

The End

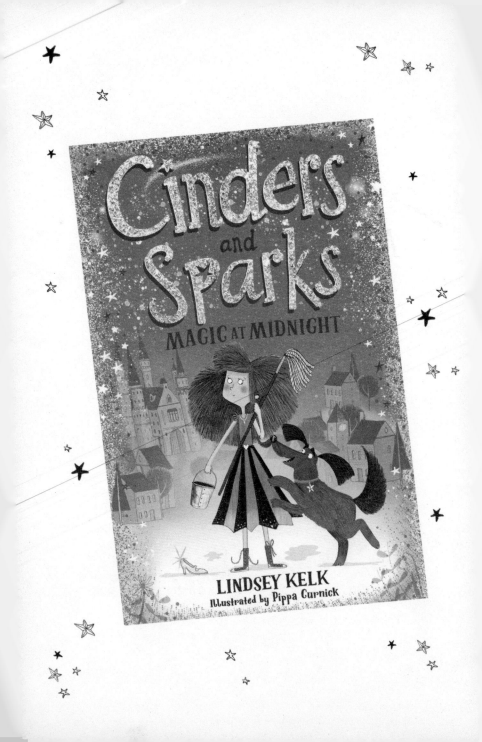

BOOK 1
MAGIC AT MIDNIGHT

Cinders lives a boring life with her selfish stepsisters and mean stepmother. So when her wishes start magically coming true it's a surprise to say the least.

Soon, Cinders finds herself heading to the glamorous ball at the king's palace. But Brian, her fairy godmother, is NOT very reliable and Cinders is NOT very good at magic. Now her life isn't boring at all – it's total chaos!

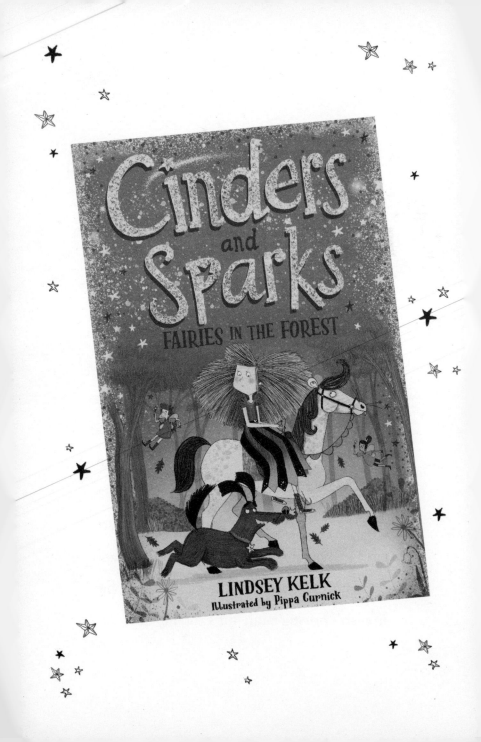

BOOK 2
FAIRIES IN THE FOREST

Cinders and her talking dog, Sparks, are fleeing fast because everyone thinks Cinders is a witch now that she's done a bit of magic. Hansel is along for the ride, but only because he ate some of an actual witch's gingerbread house and she got cross.

If they can reach Fairyland and find Cinders's mother, maybe they'll all be safe . . . or will they get more than they bargained for?